I Need a Kazoo!

by Lissa Rovetch

illustrated by Carly Castillon

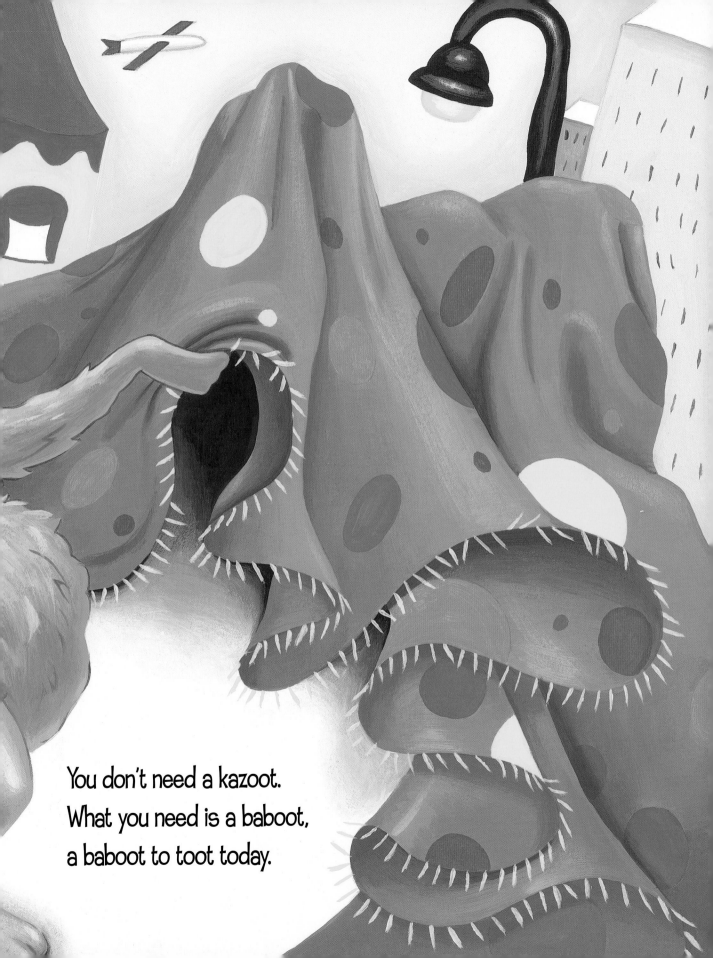

You don't need a kazoot.
What you need is a baboot,
a baboot to toot today.

A baboot is wiggly,
a baboot is loud.
If you had a baboot
you'd be so proud.

A baboot makes noises
like you never have heard.
It growls like a lion
and it tweets like a bird.

Well, that is very nice indeed,
but a kazoot is all I really need.

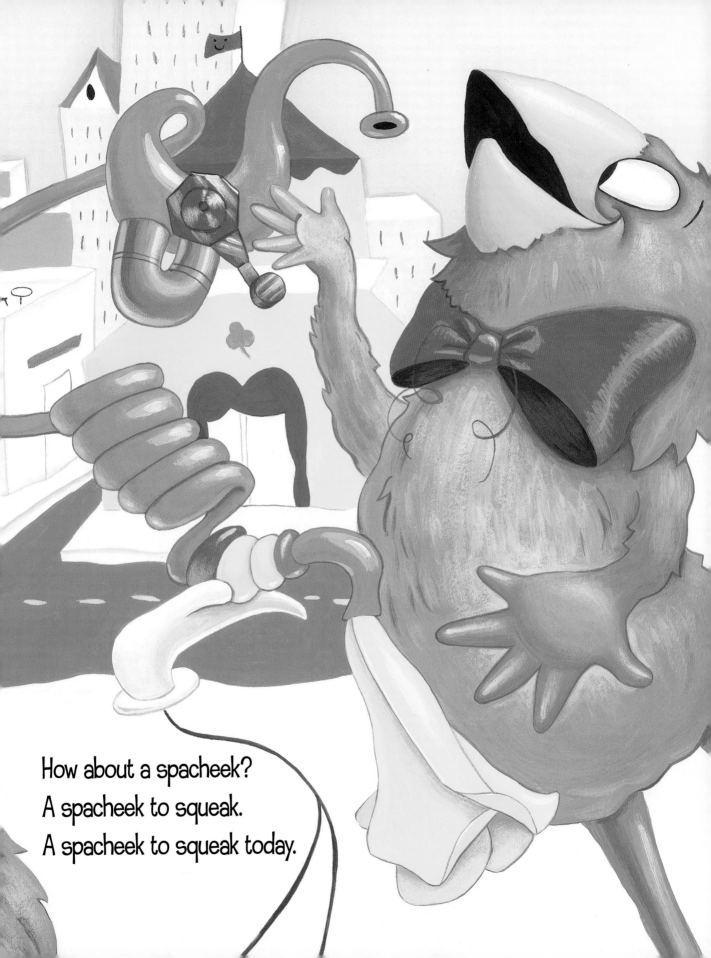

How about a spacheek?
A spacheek to squeak.
A spacheek to squeak today.

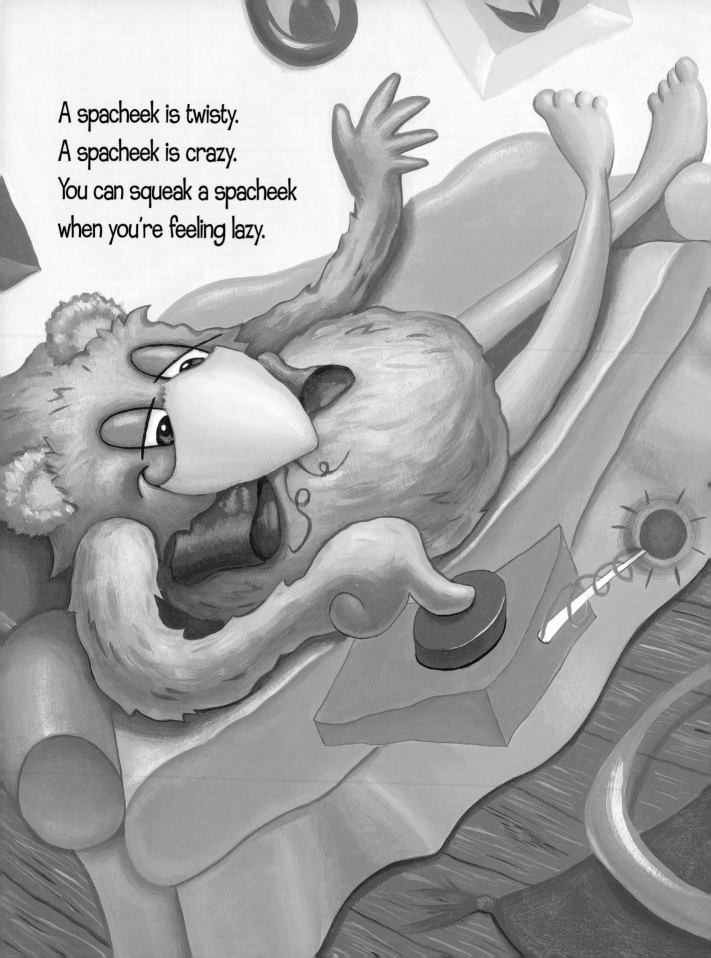

A spacheek is twisty.
A spacheek is crazy.
You can squeak a spacheek
when you're feeling lazy.

You can squeak a spacheek
in the rain and snow.
You can squeak a spacheek
anywhere that you go!

No, no, no, no.
That's not for me.
A kazoot is all I want to see.

Oh look, oh look,
I've found a zabling!
A zabling to zing today!

A zabling is stringy.
A zabling is strummy.
You can sing while you zing
this zabling on your tummy.

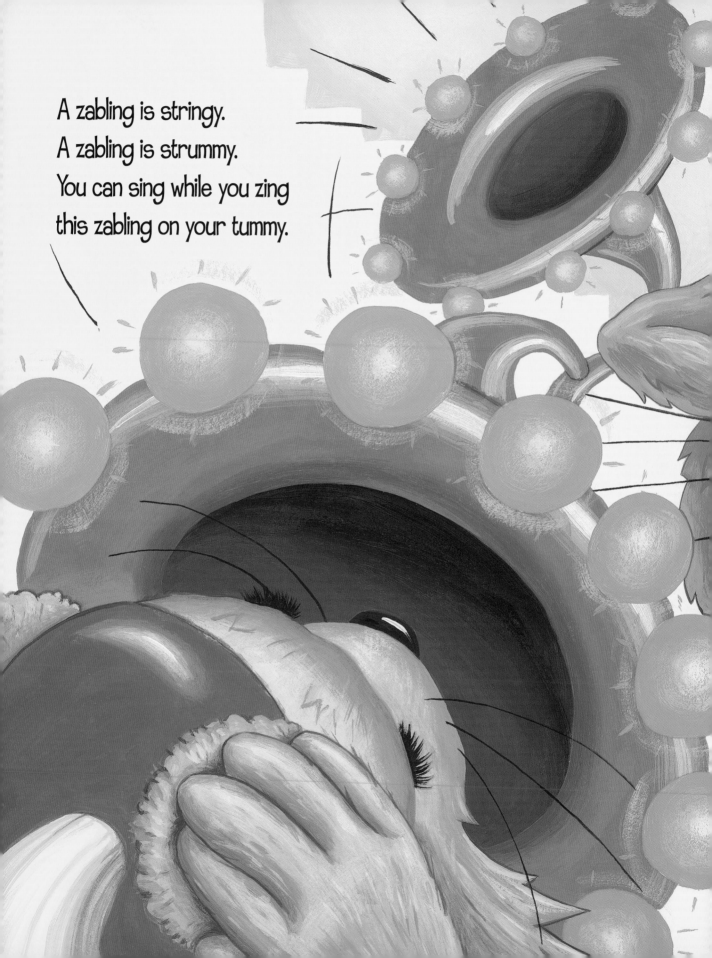

Everyone will come
from miles around,
just to hear your zabling
make its zing-a-ling sound.

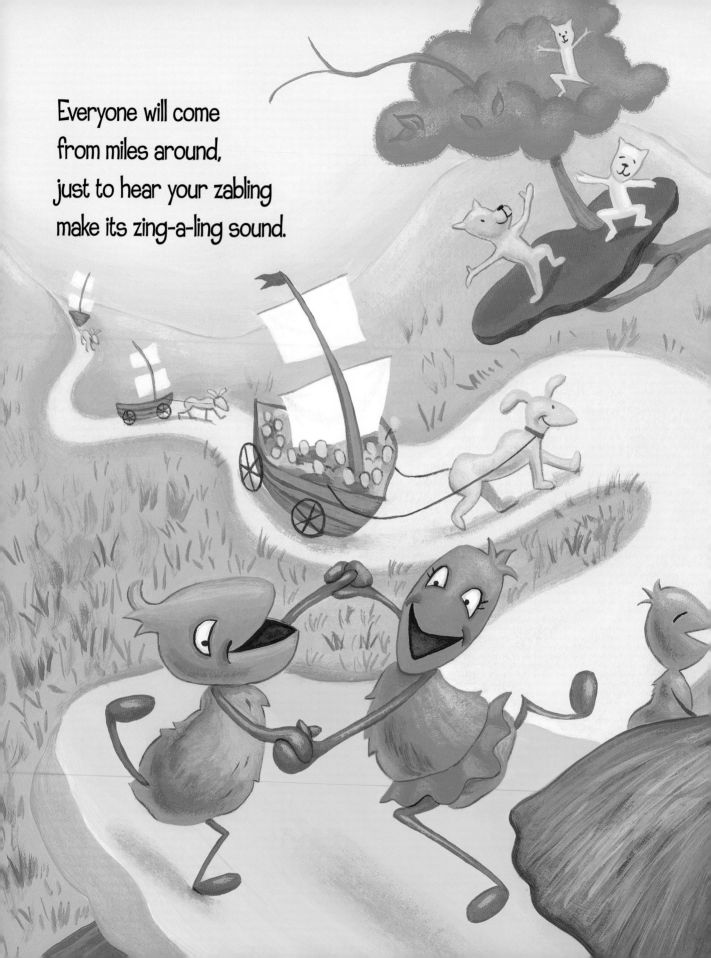

No zabling, no spacheek, and no baboot!
I'm going to go and find a kazoot!

A kazoot? A kazoot?
Why didn't you say?
I have a kazoot.
Don't go away.

This kazoot is skinny.
This kazoot is long.
This kazoot can toot
the kazoot-tootiest song!

This kazoot is perfectly
perfect for you.
It's shiny and blue
and good as new!

Thank you, thank you.
It's just right.
I'll toot this kazoot
all day and night.

These other things are fine indeed,
but this kazoot is all I need.
And once I've learned to play it well,
I might come back-
You never can tell!

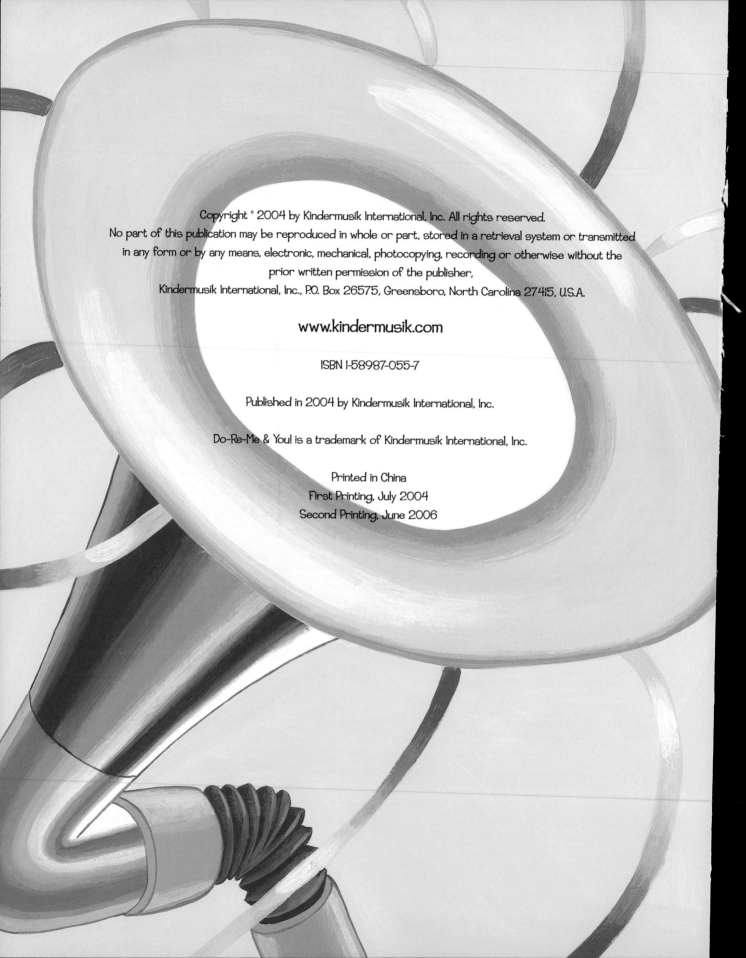

www.kindermusik.com

ISBN 1-58987-055-7

Published in 2004 by Kindermusik International, Inc.

Do-Re-Me & You! is a trademark of Kindermusik International, Inc.

Printed in China
First Printing, July 2004
Second Printing, June 2006